I AM READING

Watch Out, William!

Written and Illustrated by
KADY MACDONALD DENTON

MACMILLAN CHILDREN'S BOOKS

First published by Kingfisher 1996

This edition published 2013 by Macmillan Children's Books
a division of Macmillan Publishers Limited
20 New Wharf Road, London N1 9RR
Basingstoke and Oxford
Associated companies throughout the world
www.panmacmillan.com

ISBN 978-1-4472-0963-8

Text and illustrations copyright © Kady MacDonald Denton 1996
Educational Adviser: Prue Goodwin, Reading and Language Centre,
University of Reading

1 3 5 7 9 8 6 4 2

A CIP catalogue record for this book is available from the British Library.

Printed in China

Contents

The Walk

"You need a walk, William,"
said my sister Jane.
"No, I don't," I said.

"Yes, you do," said Jane.

"I'll come too.

We can take Pepper with us."

"I don't feel like it," I said.

"I do," said Jane,

"and I can make you

take us for a walk."

"No you can't," I said.

"I'm taller and I'm bigger."

"But you're not stronger," said Jane.

"Oh yes I am," I said.

"I'm taller and bigger and stronger."

"You're taller.

You're bigger.

But I am stronger," said Jane.

"I am so strong I can make everyone in this house come here in an instant," she added.

"So can I," I said. "Watch me."

I went and found Mum.

"Come with me," I said.

"I'm busy," said Mum.

I pulled on her chair.

I pulled and I pulled.

I pulled so hard that I dragged the chair
all the way to the living-room.

But Mum went back to work.

I found Dad.

"Come with me,"
I said.

"I'm busy," said Dad.

I tugged on his coat.

I tugged and I tugged.

I tugged so hard that I pulled that coat

all the way to the living-room.

But Dad went back to work.

I found Grandma.

"Come with me," I said.

"I'm watching TV," said Grandma.

I pushed on the bed.

I pushed and I pushed.

I pushed so hard

that the bed

almost went through the door.

But it stuck.

I found Pepper.

"Come with me," I said to the dog.

I pulled on the rug.

I pulled and I pulled.

I pulled so hard that I pulled Pepper

all the way to the living-room.

But Pepper ran away.

"Well!" said Jane.

"You have a chair, a coat and a rug,

but no people and no dog.

Now it's my turn.

Watch this!"

Jane stood still for a minute.

She took a deep breath.

Then she started to cry,

very loudly.

Before I could blink an eye –

into the room

ran Mum,

Dad,

Grandma

and Pepper the dog.

"I'm OK," said Jane.

"I'm just fine.

And *I'm* the strongest!"

Mum's face went pink.

Dad's face turned red.

Grandma turned purple.

"Out!" said Mum and Dad and Grandma.

"You both need some fresh air

before lunch."

"Yes, William," said Jane.

"We need a walk.

And we can take Pepper with us."

"Drats!" I said.

Sophie

It was a sad day

for my sister Jane.

Jane had lost her favourite toy,

her little hedgehog Sophie.

All morning she looked for Sophie.

She looked everywhere.

She looked under her bed,

under the living-room chairs

and under the rug.

She looked on top of the kitchen table,

on top of her bureau

and on top of the television.

She looked inside her clothes closet,

inside the kitchen cupboard

and inside Grandma's handbag.

Jane squeezed into the laundry basket.

But Sophie wasn't there.

25

She looked all around inside the house.

She looked all around outside the house.

No Sophie.

Mum and Dad

and Grandma and I

all helped Jane to look for Sophie.

But we didn't see

her little hedgehog anywhere.

27

Jane played with the rest of her family —

Bear, Cow and the Piglet Twins.

But Jane missed Sophie.

She started to cry.

She really cried.

"Sophie has hair to brush," sobbed Jane.

"Sophie has a face to wash."

"So do I," I said.

"Will you be my Sophie, William?

Will you be my baby?" asked Jane.

"I will if you promise

not to cry any more," I said.

Jane washed my face

and brushed my hair.

She fed me tasty treats.

"Sophie didn't really eat anything,"
said Jane.

"I did that for her."

"I eat," I said
and opened my mouth for more.

I like tasty treats.

"No more," said Jane. "It's naptime."
And she wrapped me in a blanket
and made me lie down on the sofa.
"You are supposed to go to sleep now."

"That's good," I said.

"I'd like a nice long nap.

I'm tired of rushing around looking.

I'm tired of being washed and brushed.

But this bed is too lumpy."

"Oh, dear," said Jane. "I'll be Mummy

and fix the bed for you."

She tossed the pillows onto the floor
and – look!

There was Sophie!

"Oh, Sophie" said Jane. "Here you are!

My poor little Sophie!"

"She needs her face washed

and her hair brushed," I said.

"No, William," said Jane.

"Now Sophie and I

are going to take a nap together.

We'll take a nap right here.

There's no room for you."

"Drats and rats!" I said.

The Bath

"You need a bath, William,"

said my sister Jane.

"I don't like baths," I said.

"And I don't take baths.

It's not healthy to wash all the time.

You can catch a cold that way."

"You smell," said Jane.

"Good," I said.

"You really smell," said Jane.

"Goodie, goodie!" I said
and I walked away.

Then Jane went to Dad.

"William smells," she said.

Dad laughed.

Jane went to Mum.

"William needs a bath," she said.

"Well," said Mum,

"he's old enough to take a bath

when he wants to take one."

Jane went to Grandma.

"Please, Grandma, I want a bath with lots of water."

Jane put in soap bubbles

while Grandma filled the bathtub.

She put in her boats

and her ducks

and her fish

and her octopus.

Then she put on her bathrobe.

"Oh, William!" she called.

"Oh, Will-i-am!

I'm going to take a bath.

I have bubbles and boats

and an octopus in my bath.

It's the biggest bath you ever saw."

I went to look.

"That's big," I said.

"It's for *me*," said Jane.

"It's not for you.

If you got in,

the water might go right over the top."

"Cool," I said.

"I'll try that."

Jane went out

and shut the bathroom door.

I splashed

and soaped

and made the ducks squeak.

Splish! Splash! Splosh!

Squeak!

After a long time, I came out.

"You were right, Jane," I said.

"The water did go over the top.

That bath wasn't too bad.

I might do it again.

In fact, I might go in again right now."

"No," said Jane.

"You just had a bath.

It's time for me to have *my* bath."

"Too late," I said

and for once I moved faster than Jane.

I had that bathroom door shut

before she could blink.

Splish! Splash! Splosh!

Squeak!

"Drats and rats and alleycats!" said Jane.

About the Author

Kady MacDonald Denton is one of Canada's favourite illustrators. She has written and illustrated her own picture books for very young children including *Would They Love a Lion?* published by Kingfisher. Kady says, "I got the first idea for William and Jane from remembering my own childhood. I used to think that my younger brother was far too little to fool me and so, of course, I was never prepared for all his tricks. But sometimes I turned the tables on him – just like William does."

Tips for Beginner Readers

1. Think about the cover and the title of the book. What do you think it will be about? While you are reading, think about what might happen next and why.

2. As you read, ask yourself if what you're reading makes sense. If it doesn't, try rereading or look at the pictures for clues.

3. If there is a word that you do not know, look carefully at the letters, sounds, and word parts that you do know. Blend the sounds to read the word. Is this a word you know? Does it make sense in the sentence?

4. Think about the characters, where the story takes place, and the problems the characters in the story faced. What are the important ideas in the beginning, middle and end of the story?

5. Ask yourself questions like:
> Did you like the story?
> Why or why not?
> How did the author make it fun to read?
> How well did you understand it?

Maybe you can understand the story better if you read it again!